MILLIE MAGNUS
★ FOR MAYOR ★

**ALSO STARRING
MILLIE MAGNUS AND FRIENDS**

Millie Magnus Won't Be Bullied

MILLIE MAGNUS
★ FOR MAYOR ★

BRITTANY MAZIQUE
ILLUSTRATED BY EBONY GLENN

putnam

G. P. PUTNAM'S SONS

G. P. PUTNAM'S SONS
An imprint of Penguin Random House LLC
1745 Broadway, New York, NY 10019

First published in the United States of America by G. P. Putnam's Sons, 2025

Text copyright © 2025 by Brittany Mazique
Illustrations copyright © 2025 by Ebony Glenn

Penguin Random House values and supports copyright. Copyright fuels creativity, encourages diverse voices, promotes free speech, and creates a vibrant culture. Thank you for buying an authorized edition of this book and for complying with copyright laws by not reproducing, scanning, or distributing any part of it in any form without permission. You are supporting writers and allowing Penguin Random House to continue to publish books for every reader. Please note that no part of this book may be used or reproduced in any manner for the purpose of training artificial intelligence technologies or systems.

G. P. Putnam's Sons is a registered trademark of Penguin Random House LLC.
The Penguin colophon is a registered trademark of Penguin Books Limited.

Visit us online at PenguinRandomHouse.com.

Library of Congress Cataloging-in-Publication Data
Names: Mazique, Brittany, author. | Glenn, Ebony, illustrator.
Title: Millie Magnus for mayor / Brittany Mazique; illustrated by Ebony Glenn.
Description: New York: G. P. Putnam's Sons, 2025. | Summary: "Millie Magnus learns what not to do when she tries to lead her friends in an effort to save their neighborhood playground from being torn down"—Provided by publisher.
Identifiers: LCCN 2024002558 (print) | LCCN 2024002559 (ebook) | ISBN 9780593618806 (hardcover) | ISBN 9780593618813 (trade paperback) | ISBN 9780593618820 (epub)
Subjects: CYAC: Behavior–Fiction. | Leadership–Fiction. | Playgrounds–Fiction.
Classification: LCC PZ7.1.M393 Mh 2025 (print) | LCC PZ7.1.M393 (ebook) | DDC [Fic]–dc23
LC record available at https://lccn.loc.gov/2024002558
LC ebook record available at https://lccn.loc.gov/2024002559

Manufactured in the United States of America
LSCC
ISBN 9780593618806 (hardcover)
1st Printing
ISBN 9780593618813 (paperback)
1st Printing

Design by Suki Boynton • Text set in Modum

The authorized representative in the EU for product safety and compliance is Penguin Random House Ireland, Morrison Chambers, 32 Nassau Street, Dublin D02 YH68, Ireland, https://eu-contact.penguin.ie.

*To every young leader in
the making—lead with love, listen
with care, and make room for all.*
—B.M.

CONTENTS

1. Bad News Bearers — 1
2. The Real Chill Deal — 15
3. Mayor See, Mayor Do — 31
4. One for All, or All for None? — 40
5. Sunday Afternoon Blues — 53
6. Extra Pressing News — 61
7. Icky, Sticky Bubble Gums — 68
8. The Cheese Stands Alone — 75
9. S-O-R-R-Y, I'm Sorry — 82
10. Can't Judge a Book — 87
11. No Rain, No Rainbows — 100
12. All Together Now! — 116

1
Bad News Bearers

"MILLICENT MAGNUS MILLER!"

I dip my brush into a pot of bright orange and keep on painting. "Busy!" I yell back from under Mayor Maude's desk. One: because I am busy. And two: because Josephine Draper knows I mostly go by Millie Magnus.

"BAWK!" That's what my pet chicken, Extra Spicy, says when he sticks a foot into purple paint and steps onto our paper.

Today we are making Mayor Maude a picture to hang in her home office. She needs one! Right now, this room is the colors of not-so-interesting foods. Like oatmeal. And wheat bread. But it won't be once we're done, on account of Extra Spicy and I are artists. And that we don't like anything plain or boring.

I get a whiff of old leather. Then I see Josephine Draper's feet.

"Millicent Magnus, I declare! Chickens have no business painting. And certainly NOT in the mayor's office."

That Josephine Draper has been bothering me ever since I woke up this morning. That's when she wanted me to wear the itchy, ruffly pajamas she picked out for mismatched pajama day on the last day of school.

"Mismatched pajama day is supposed to be fun, not itchy and ruffly!" I told her. That's why I'm wearing my favorite doughnut-and-taco pajamas—with the matching top and bottom on account of *that's* mismatched for me.

Josephine Draper places a tray with two coffee cups on a table in Mayor Maude's office. Extra Spicy raises an eyebrow, and I do, too.

"Who's the extra cup for?" I ask.

"Mayor Maude's new architect, Mr. Longfellow." She picks up Extra Spicy and wipes a big glob of purple paint off his claws. "I'm afraid you and dear Extra Spicy will have to take your art elsewhere."

Sometimes Josephine Draper confuses being Mayor Maude's assistant with being the boss of me. Here's a piece of news: She's not. I crawl out from under the desk and take Extra Spicy in my arms. "This office needs some color," I say.

"Is that so?" Josephine Draper asks. Then she points out the window. "Mayor Maude is pulling into the driveway!

Hurry and pack away your paints and get Extra Spicy to his coop!"

My ears try to listen to what Josephine Draper is saying, but Extra Spicy is busy squirming out of my arms and my nose is too busy sniffing something yucky from the kitchen. Mayor Maude walks into the office before I can ask what the smell is.

I run and leap into her arms. "My favorite mayor!" I say, resting my cheek next to hers.

"How about favorite *mom*," she says back. Mayor Maude doesn't mind being called Mayor Maude by everyone else in Washington, DC. But when it comes to me, she'd rather just be Mom.

My cheeks get a little warm and a tiny

bit red, too. "My favorite *mooooom*," I say back.

Mayor Maude puts me down and motions to the man with her. "Millie Magnus," she says, "can you say hello to Mr. Longfellow?"

I look up. Then up and up and up. This Longfellow guy is so tall, he looks like his legs were stretched out and then attached to his body!

"Wow!" I say. "I bet you were the tallest guy in your class."

Mr. Longfellow smiles. Then stoops down to my level, which if you didn't know is pretty close to the ground for a guy like him. "Nice to finally meet you, Millie Magnus," he says. "I've heard so much about you."

I tilt my head back and point my nose to the sky. Then I put my hand on my hip and say, "Mostly good, I'm sure!"

Mr. Longfellow laughs before he walks over to a private room in Mayor Maude's office. That room is reserved for two things. The first is me. I go in there and take some time to myself in the reading nook when I need a break from Josephine Draper. The other thing is important conversations. That must be why Mr. Longfellow is here.

Just when I start wondering what he's going to talk to Mayor Maude about, my brain goes back to remembering Extra Spicy. I think he's under Mayor Maude's desk with the paint!

"Oh boy!" I say to myself.

When I need to get from one side of the room to the other FAST, I give myself a little run and then slide the rest of the way on my knees.

Most times, this is a great idea. Today I'm not so sure. I slide down and stop right under Mayor Maude's desk just as Extra

Spicy runs across our painting with rainbow claws. I catch him before he can land on Mayor Maude's coconut-colored carpet. I act natural, like everything is fine, just in time to ask Mayor Maude about dinner.

"Mom?"

She peeks her head under the desk. "Millie Magnus?"

"You promised to make tuna casserole tonight. It's Friday, and we always have tuna casserole on Fridays."

"I suppose *this* leopard never changes her spots, now does she?" she says.

I'm not sure what that means. But I don't spend too much time trying to figure it out.

Because that's when the smell from the kitchen somersaults into my nostrils again and I can tell it's Josephine Draper's barbecue chicken and yucky deviled eggs. I wish I could plug my nose with my paintbrushes. There's no way I'm eating Josephine Draper's dinner.

In case you didn't know, I don't eat eggs no matter how they're cooked. And neither does Extra Spicy. For good reason!

Mayor Maude wipes some paint off of my cheek with her thumb. "Change can feel really scary before you try something new. But if you just give change a chance, you'll see things usually have a way of turning out okay, and maybe even good in the end."

I can imagine Josephine Draper's dinner being lots of things. Good is not one of them.

Mayor Maude stands up to join Mr. Longfellow in the important conversation room. I squint my eyes to see through the tiny window in the door. I press my whole body on that door to try to hear what Mr. Longfellow is saying.

"BAWK!" squawks Extra Spicy.

"BRRRRRRIIIINNNGGG!" rings Mayor Maude's phone.

"OH MILLICENT MAGNUS MILLER! DINNERRRRRRRR!" Josephine Draper calls from the kitchen.

"Coming!" I shout back sweetly. But really, I'm trying to hear what Mayor Maude is saying. Something about our neighborhood playground. Mr. Longfellow pulls out a blueprint.

In case you don't know, a blueprint is a

big flat drawing that looks fancy. Actually, it's just a bunch of shapes and lines.

I know because I've seen blueprints before. Mayor Maude, my dad, and I drew one together when we tore down the shed in our backyard so we could build a chicken coop. Building the coop was one of the last things we did before he died.

Mayor Maude still has that blueprint hanging in a frame in her office. And a picture of the three of us in front of the coop after we put the final touches on it

is right on her desk. Seeing them makes me sad. In my mind, I change the channel because there's an important conversation I need to hear.

I lean my ear on the door to the room where Mayor Maude and Mr. Longfellow are sitting. I hear a few words I wish I hadn't.

"Tear down..."

"Playground..."

"Change it to..."

But before I can hear the rest, I see paint dripping from Extra Spicy's feet and imagine him moonwalking all across Mayor Maude's rice-colored couch.

I scream two times.

First, because Extra Spicy is going to get in big trouble!

Second, because I think I just heard some really awful news. They're going to destroy the neighborhood playground. I love that playground more than anything. It's where I go to have fun with all my friends. It's also where someone super special used to take me before he was gone forever.

I pick up Extra Spicy in one hand and the picture frame from Mayor Maude's desk in the other. I remember how Mayor Maude and Dad held a ribbon across the door to the coop and I got to cut it. We looked so happy that day, before everything changed.

I can't let this playground be something else that changes, too.

2
The Real Chill Deal

PSSSSSSSSHHHHHHHHHHHH!

I close my eyes tight as I slip down my favorite slide on the playground, straight into a cloud of bug spray. "Thank you, Lunchbox. I think that's enough." I cough. Lunchbox's grandma agrees before taking the bottle of bug spray and finding a seat on the bench to do a crossword puzzle.

"On a hot, damp day like today, you can never be too sure." He checks his arms for bites. "Trust me. It's like paradise for mosquitos." He places his lunch box on the ground in front of the giant pirate ship swing set.

Lunchbox sits down, and there's a loud *crunch*. He jumps right back up and gives his lunch box a good look. That lunch box goes everywhere he goes. And it's always full of stuff. Some useful. Some not so much. Like his collection of shoelaces or his dog's chew toy.

I look at my wrist to check the time. That's when I remember I'm not wearing a watch.

"Where are Atticus and Poppy Anne?" I whine. "We've been waiting MINUTES!" Which feels like forever when you have big news to tell your friends.

"What's so serious we had to get here right away, anyway?" Lunchbox asks.

My hands feel like slime, and my stomach can't sit still. I pace on the balance beam. "It's really important I tell everyone all at once."

"It must be big if you skipped Greta Perez and the Real Chill Pickles' fashion show," says Lunchbox.

"Oh boy," I sigh, and cover my eyes. I was so upset about the terrible news I heard in Mayor Maude's office that I completely forgot what day it is.

"It's Friday, isn't it?" I say with a little more sadness.

"Yep! You'll never be picked to be in the show if you can't even remember when it is!" says Lunchbox.

Greta Perez is my cool fourth-grade next-door neighbor. And everyone loves everything about her. Including me. Greta and the Real Chill Pickles are just like me and my friends, the Moody Bubble Gums. Only older. And cooler, too.

My friends are walking toward us from the wooden stage at the edge of the playground. I wave at them to move faster.

"Sorry we're late," says Poppy Anne. She skips over to the pirate ship like she's just awakened from a good dream. Meanwhile, I'm living a bad one. "You'll never guess the supercool thing Greta Perez just did!" she gushes.

Usually I'd make lots of time to fan over Greta Perez. But not today. Only, Poppy Anne is one of my best friends

and the kindest person I know. So I try to listen.

"Fine. What were the Real Chill Pickles doing today?" I ask. Because that's the nice thing to do. Plus, I really want to know.

Poppy Anne can hardly keep a lid on her excitement. "You won't believe it, Millie Magnus." Even Lunchbox leans in closer.

"She's wearing my mom's design! You know the lilac jumpsuit with the lightning bolts and ruffly sleeves?!"

I do know the one. It's the exact one I wanted. Only Josephine Draper said it didn't come in my size. Which is probably Josephine Draper talk for *it's not fancy enough.*

Poppy Anne's mom is a fashion designer. But her designs aren't the Josephine Draper fancy kind. They are the Millie Magnus cool kind.

"I can't believe it! Greta Perez wearing one of my mom's jumpsuits is better than being famous!"

"She's got a point," says Lunchbox. Atticus high-fives Poppy Anne.

Usually, I'd be super happy to talk about jumpsuits, ruffly sleeves, and lightning bolt patterns. But right now I can't stop thinking about the playground and what is about to happen to it. I feel a bubble swell in my tummy right before it comes out as a giant hiccup. Then the words come leaping out of my mouth.

"They're going to destroy the playground!" I shout as I jump down from the balance beam and land next to Atticus.

"Our playground?" he asks.

"Who's going to?" questions Lunchbox.

Poppy Anne's mouth falls open. "Why would anyone want to do that?"

I take a deep breath. "I overheard Mayor Maude and this tall guy, Mr. Longshmellow, talking about it."

Lunchbox lowers his eyebrows. "Are you *sure* that's what you heard?"

"Of course she is," says Poppy Anne. "This is awful."

I look around our playground and imagine this pirate ship as a sunken one. "They'll probably build a fancy apartment building. Maybe a dog park. Or some organic vegetable market." I shut my eyes at the thought of it. I don't like vegetables. Especially cauliflower.

But they don't stay closed long. That's because I smell cherry blossoms and birthday cake. There's only one person I know who smells like that.

"Oh, hey, Greta!" I say. I nod at her BFFs, Izzie and Chance.

The Real Chill Pickles are standing right in front of me in one of those older-kid poses. The kind where they look like they stand that way naturally, but it probably takes lots of practice. I know because I've tried it before. Couldn't do it.

Greta is wearing the lightning bolt jumpsuit and a thick stack of beaded friendship bracelets. Izzie has on a sequin jacket that sparkles and shines. Chance is wearing shorts that match Greta's jumpsuit. His sneakers light up. In case you can't tell by now, these Pickles are cool.

"What's the deal, Mills?" That's short for Millie. And cool older-kid talk for "Hey, kid. How's it going?"

Before I can stop myself, I shout, "THE PLAYGROUND IS GOING AWAY FOREVER!"

Greta's cool-girl pose changes. And I know it's because she heard what I said, loud and clear!

"No way," says Greta. "Where would we all come to hang out? What would happen to, like, our Friday fashion shows?"

"Well." Lunchbox pulls a bottle of tomato juice out of his lunch box and takes a sip. "It depends on what they put here instead."

"Lunchbox!" I cry out. "Don't say that!

This playground isn't going anywhere if I have anything to do with it." I sound braver than I actually feel.

"I'm with Millie Magnus," says Greta. "But if we're going to save the playground, we need a plan. And a leader. Like a president or a mayor. Someone needs to be in charge of saving the playground."

At first, this sounds pretty silly to me. Mayors lead *people*, not kids who want to save a playground. But after a few seconds, I start to believe Greta's idea isn't so bad. "Well, if we're looking for a mayor, I'm the girl for the job!" I say, standing up tall.

"The mayor should be Greta," suggests Chance. "She's the oldest."

"But my mom is the real mayor of this

city, so I have the most experience," I add. I've watched Mayor Maude for most of my life. Phone calls, photo ops, speeches, ribbon cuttings for grand openings—I know how to do all that stuff.

"Just because your mom is mayor doesn't mean it would make *you* the right person for the job, Millie Magnus. This is a big problem. And it will require BIG ideas to solve it," says Greta. "I've planned lots of fashion shows, and there's always something unexpected popping up. Plus, I'm older and have been coming to this playground the longest, so it matters more to me."

Greta may be older. And she may be the best fashion show planner. But there's nobody, and I mean nobody, who wants to save this playground more than I do.

I walk right up to that Greta Perez. "I'm the one who found out about this tearing-down-the-playground business! So that means *I* should be mayor." Then

I put my hands on my hips. "I'll save this place if it's the last thing I do as mayor!"

Everyone looks at one another, but no one says a word except Greta.

"Well, you heard her, everyone," says Greta. "Millie Magnus is our new mayor.

As long as we work together, we should be able to save the playground."

Wow! That was easier than I thought.

I let out a big breath, then say, "Let's get to work!" It's my first sentence as the official mayor.

See? I'm already off to a great start. How hard can this mayor business be, anyway?

3
Mayor See, Mayor Do

Here's a piece of interesting news: Figuring out how to be the leader of this whole saving-the-playground thing is hard. A lot harder than I thought it would be. I need ideas and FAST!

The good news is I know just the place to brainstorm: Mayor Maude's office. What better place to think like a mayor than at an actual mayor's desk?

This is an advantage Greta Perez would NOT have!

I open my purple notebook covered in stickers. I pick up my favorite orange-scented marker. Only it doesn't write so well anymore. I must have forgotten to put the cap back on tight. I grab one of Mayor Maude's pens instead.

Mayor Maude plops down in a chair in front of her desk. Which makes me feel even more like a real mayor. She slides off her shoes and lets out a deep sigh. The *I'm happy to be home with Millie Magnus* kind.

"Long day?" I ask.

"*Very*," she says back.

"It's not easy being mayor. Trust me. I know."

Mayor Maude smiles big. "You don't say?"

Yep. Actually, I did say that.

I know Mayor Maude is tired. But I can't waste any time trying to figure out what a mayor would do in my shoes.

"Mom, how does a leader get something done when everyone is counting on them?"

Mayor Maude sits up straight and puts on her serious face. "That's a really good question. And the answer depends."

I lean across her desk and wait for her answer.

"I make a plan," says Mayor Maude.

"A plan?"

"Yes, a plan. Lots of leaders start with one," she says.

"What if your plan sort of looks like this . . . ?" I hold up the blank page in my purple notebook.

Mayor Maude flashes me a small smile. "That happens more than you think. When it does, I brainstorm with my team. Two heads are better than one. You know what I mean?"

Mayor Maude can tell by the shape of my eyebrows that I don't understand what she means.

"In other words, it's easier for more people to come together to solve a problem than it is for someone to go about it alone."

That makes better sense. Next time, Mayor Maude should just say that instead. "And that works?" I ask.

"It has for me."

"Even with, let's say . . . kids. Some older. And some younger. But all cool. Of course."

"Of course," Mayor Maude agrees.

"Well, it should. As long as it doesn't seem like there are too many cooks in the kitchen."

This doesn't make sense to me, either. But I'll tell you one cook who should never be in the kitchen. And that's Josephine Draper.

"What does cooking have to do with being a good leader?" I ask.

Mayor Maude's shoulders shake with laughter. "It's a saying. It means there are too many people in charge instead of one person. But a good leader knows how to listen and communicate so everyone feels like they're part of the solution, and they work together as a team."

I write down one person in charge in my notebook and close it. "Thanks, Mayor

Maude. I do have one more question for you."

"I'm all ears," she says.

"Well, I heard you and that tall guy, Mr. Longfellow, talking the other day and—"

But before I can get the rest of the words out, Josephine Draper barges into the room with a stack of papers.

"If I may, Mayor Maude?" she says. "Your signature here... and here... and... here."

Mayor Maude signs the papers. Then Josephine Draper picks them up and rushes out of the room. I write **signing lots of papers** in my notebook.

Mayor Maude puts down her pen. "Go on, Millie Magnus."

"And I know what the city is planning on doing to the playground. And I want to know—"

In comes that Josephine Draper again! "Pardon me again, Mayor Maude, but you have a call. Should I have them call you back?"

I give Mayor Maude my best *pretty please* look.

"Yes, Josephine. Please do. I need just a few more minutes with Millie Magnus."

"Certainly, Mayor Maude."

"Now, where were we?" Mayor Maude asks.

"Why would the city want to get rid of a perfectly good playground? It's the place where I—"

"I hate to interrupt again," interrupts

Josephine Draper. "But you must take this call. It's urgent."

"I'm so sorry, Millie Magnus. Let's talk about this a little later." Mayor Maude stands up and walks toward the important conversation room. She turns around and blows me a kiss. I catch it and press it to my cheek.

I pick up my marker and notebook. Saving the playground is too important. I don't have time to wait for Mayor Maude to explain. I've got mayor stuff to do.

Lots of stuff!

One for All, or All for None?

"How's that?" I move Extra Spicy's desk a little closer to mine.

"BAWK!" he squawks. Which means he approves.

Any minute now, the Moody Bubble Gums and the Real Chill Pickles will all be in my new mayoral office. Which is just a fancy word for an office for a mayor. And mine happens to be in Extra Spicy's coop.

Extra Spicy and I stayed up almost

all night making sure the office was just right.

We picked out pictures of me where I look the most in charge and hung them on the walls—kind of like the ones Mayor Maude has in her office.

I put up one from when I won the chili-eating contest. (Here's a secret tip: Crumble gingersnaps on top.) And the one when I almost won the science fair instead of Lunchbox. He shared his certificate with me. So he has his half, and now my half hangs behind my desk.

I turned an old box into a mayor's desk. With a nice layer of orange paint, it looks good as new.

I hear voices and then footsteps on the stoop of the coop. I push a few papers under my desk and give my office a final look. I pinch my fingers to my thumbs and kiss them. "Chef's kiss!" I say, tossing the kiss to the air.

I glance in my purple notebook one last time and read in big bold letters: One person in charge. This is going to be a piece of cake.

"BAWK!"

"Is that Extra Spicy?" I hear Chance ask behind the door.

"Does she really have a pet chicken?" Izzie asks.

"Sure does," I hear Lunchbox say.

"That's so cool," whispers Greta.

I beam. This is off to a great start already.

As soon as everyone is inside, I put them right to work! "Time to make posters!"

I start telling everyone what to do. "Lunchbox, did you bring the markers? Atticus, grab that stack of poster boards. Write *Kids for Playgrounds* as big as you can!"

"What about something that explains what's happening?" suggests Lunchbox.

"Like what?" I ask. But I don't wait to hear his answer. "Bigger letters, Atticus!"

"How about we write ways people can help

us on the posters!" suggests Greta.

Everyone makes a bunch of noise cheering the idea. But I don't.

"Real Chills . . . less chilling and more working!" I bark.

"Millie Magnus." Poppy Anne puts her hand on my shoulder. This usually means she thinks I need to pump my brakes!

"Too fast?" I ask.

"More like . . . too bossy," she whispers.

"Poppy Anne, I'm the mayor. Of a very important cause . . . the playground!!! I think we can all agree that it's one of our favorite places to go together as a group. It's going to be destroyed in a matter of who-knows-when!" I say in a loud whisper.

"Yeah, but we're supposed to be working together on a plan. It seems like you've already decided what we're doing."

I stand up from my desk. "That reminds me. Greta?" I shout to the other side of the coop. "Let's not use the glitter. Extra Spicy will only track it everywhere. It'll be a disaster."

"Oh. Sorry." Greta puts down the glitter and picks up a hot-pink marker.

"Hot pink?" I ask. "We need colors that can be seen a mile away." I toss her a dark green marker. "Try this one!"

Greta catches the marker and shoots Chance a look. "Here's the deal, Millie Magnus. Saving the playground is important to all of us. So, like, let us decide how we want to decorate our posters, too."

Atticus nods and picks up the jar of glitter.

I squint my eyes at him. He squints his back.

"Fine. But there's a right way to do this and there's a wrong way. Trust me, I know."

"Just because your mom is mayor doesn't mean you know everything," says Izzie. I ignore this. Mostly because I don't think I know everything. But I do think I know how to be mayor.

"So, what's our plan after we make posters?" asks Poppy Anne.

Only I don't know what we're going to do next.

"How about we post them around the neighborhood?" suggests Chance.

"That's a great idea!" adds Greta. I think it's a pretty all right idea.

"Maybe, Chance. But I was thinking of something more GRAND than that."

Greta lets out a deep sigh. "Like what, Millie Magnus?"

That's when the clippity-cloppity of Josephine Draper's heels hits my ears. I'm actually happy that lady is coming. One, because I don't have a good answer for Greta. And two, because of her plate of snacks!

"Helloooooo?" she calls through the window.

"Not right now, Josephine Draper," I say, taking the snacks and handing them out to my friends. "We're really busy."

"Too busy to hear something *cool* I need to tell you?"

"Maybe later, okay?" I decide this is the most polite thing to say. I'd never want to embarrass someone in front of the Real Chill Pickles. Not even Josephine Draper.

That's when Extra Spicy does it again. He steps right into the jar of glitter and flies all around the coop, dropping clumps of glitter like little parachutes from his claws.

Everyone throws their arms in the air, running underneath each little cloud of glitter like they want to catch it in their hair.

"You guys! That's enough! Extra Spicy, stop it!" This is no way to behave in a mayor's office! I run to pick up the other jars of glitter before Extra Spicy can put his sparkly claws in any more of them!

"Millie Magnus, just chill. We're just, like, having a good time," says Greta.

"Yeah, have a little fun," says Chance.

"Fun?" My voice begins to shake. But

only just a little. "The city is about to destroy the one place we can all go in the neighborhood to have fun! And all you guys want to do is play in glitter with my pet chicken!"

"BAWK!"

I ignore Extra Spicy.

"Well, at least your pet chicken is more fun than some bossy kid mayor." Greta Perez walks toward the door. She turns and looks at me. "Here's the deal, Millie Magnus. You and the Moodies can go save the playground by yourselves. We're out of here!" She turns to Izzie and Chance. "C'mon."

They follow behind her.

"Good luck on your own," says Izzie.

Chance slams the door behind them, and one of my pictures falls off the wall.

"Great," I say, picking it up.

Lunchbox uses a wet wipe to clean the glitter off his face. "What are we going to do now?" he asks.

"The same as before," I say, crossing my arms. "We're saving the playground, even if it's the last thing I do as mayor." Then I look at my friends.

Atticus, Lunchbox, and Poppy Anne all look glum.

I square my shoulders. "Don't worry," I say. "The Real Chill Pickles will be back."

At least I hope they will be.

5

Sunday Afternoon Blues

The Real Chill Pickles are NOT coming back.

I find this out the hard way.

I'm in my office with Lunchbox, Poppy Anne, and Atticus. We're making a pretend playground out of LEGOs. Poster boards are all around us. I'm telling them about plans—real playground-saving plans!

"Millie Magnus, how is this LEGO

playground going to help us save the real thing?"

I am in the middle of pacing when Poppy Anne asks this. I stop dead in my tracks because I'm not sure how it's going to help us honestly. But I don't tell my friends that.

"Every mayor has mini buildings of their town in their office, Poppy Anne. It's the only way a *real* mayor—"

There's a knock on the window. Izzie hands an envelope to Lunchbox. It has my name in big letters, so he passes it to me. I sit down at my desk and open the neon-orange cheetah-print envelope. The letter is on matching paper with Greta's name in the perfect pop of hot pink on top.

I start reading aloud to my friends.

GRETA PEREZ

TO WHOM THIS MAY CONCERN:
While the playground has been the center of some of our most famous moments, like the award-winning Real Chill Pickles Fashion Shows (to name one), we (Greta Perez, Izzie Applebottom, and Chance Johnson) have decided we no longer would like to partner with the Moody Bubble Gums under the bossy leadership of a made-up mayor like Millie Magnus Miller (who we have come to discover is really named Millicent Magnus Miller). We wish the Moody Bubble Gums well in their playground-saving journey. A journey, after much soul-searching overnight, we have come to realize we are too old to care about.

Hope you understand the deal,
Greta Perez (A Real Chill Pickle)

I bang my fist on the desk. "How dare she?" I huff. "Made-up mayor?"

I begin to pace again, hoping my face isn't as red as my insides. "And WHO told her my real name? I'm MILLIE MAGNUS!" I shout.

Lunchbox takes a napkin out of his lunch box and cleans his glasses. "Let me see the letter."

I hand it to him and keep pacing.

"So what do we do now?" asks Atticus. His eyes look worried.

This makes me worried, too. But I don't say it out loud. Instead, I say, "We keep fighting! It's too important to give up now."

"There must be something we can do, Millie Magnus. We *need* the Real Chill

Pickles," says Lunchbox. "Write them back. Or invite Greta over and see if we can change their minds."

I laugh off the idea. "Well, that's a silly suggestion. More working and less worrying about Greta and her Pickles!"

"No, Millie Magnus. You aren't getting it." Poppy Anne takes the letter out of Lunchbox's hand and points at it. "You upset the Real Chill Pickles. Greta may sound all cool in this letter. But I think you hurt their feelings."

Now I'm positive my face is as red as my insides. "Hurt their feelings?"

"Yeah. You bossed everyone around. You wouldn't listen to anyone else's ideas. Then you screamed at everyone when we were all just trying to have fun."

Poppy Anne is firm. Which I think is bossy.

"You should apologize," she says.

The corners of Lunchbox's mouth are drawn down. Atticus's eyebrows are scrunched so close, they look knitted together. I know the faces of my friends very well. And I know this means they agree with Poppy Anne.

But I don't know what to tell them. I can hardly *think* about not having the playground anymore. How could I even explain to my friends what not having the playground anymore would mean to me? I look away from them before I cry. That's when I see my notebook on my desk and remember who's in charge.

"Let's get back to work," I say, because it's the only thing my mind can think of.

Really my heart wants to tell them the actual reason the playground means so much to me.

It was the place I used to go with my dad. We had so much fun there together.

Everything changed after he passed away. Which is why I don't want any more changes. Especially when it comes to the playground.

I wish those words would come tumbling out of my mouth.

But I can't seem to make them.

6

Extra Pressing News

I sit up in bed and yawn. It's morning outside my window. But I'm still tired. Not a good way to start the first Monday of summer vacation if you ask me.

I hardly got any sleep last night trying to do all the work no one was around to help with. I had to finish all the posters to go up around the playground. Plus, the pretend playground my friends made of

LEGOs looked nothing like the real thing. So I had to take it all apart and start all over again.

And I wrote a speech.

I'm not exactly sure when I will need it. But one thing I know about mayors is they're always giving speeches. Plus, the speech I wrote is an important one.

It may be the best way to tell everyone how I really feel about the playground going away. If I read it, maybe I'll be able to get the words out.

I push back the covers and hop out of bed.

I walk to my closet, my eyes barely open, and put on the first things I find. Lucky for me, it's my favorite polka-dot poodle T-shirt and a skirt. I pair them with my pink cheetah rain boots. It's the best I can do on such little sleep. I pick up the posters scattered around my room and stuff them in one of Mayor Maude's re-usable grocery bags.

Before I leave my room, I take a look at Extra Spicy lying in his bed. I want to be upset with him about the whole glitter thing from the other day. But I can't imagine being mad at him. He's just a sweet chicken.

I tuck him snuggly tight under the covers and whisper in his ears, "Extra Spicy, no mischief today. Mayor Millie Magnus has a playground to save."

I'm ready to head to the playground to hang posters. That's when I hear a voice that sounds a lot like that Longfellow guy.

Then a laugh. It *is* Mr. Longfellow. Then I hear Mayor Maude laughing, too.

"What's so funny?" I ask myself. "And what's Mr. Longfellow doing in Mayor Maude's office this early in the morning?"

I tiptoe down really quickly. When I get to the hallway outside the office, I press myself against the big pink and cream flowers on the wallpaper. My

cheetah-print rain boots are perfect for blending in.

"Thanks, Johnny," I hear Mayor Maude say to Mr. Longfellow. "I think we have everything we need for a fantastic press conference."

Press conference!

If you don't know . . . a press conference is where newspeople bring their biggest microphones and cameras and stand outside waiting for Mayor Maude to show up to speak. Josephine Draper is always reminding me not to do anything silly in front of those cameras. And I tell her not to, either.

"I'm glad you're happy with the plans, Maude. I think this is going to be a great addition to the community. And Millie will be happy, too!"

If I weren't so busy being invisible, I'd remind Mr. Longfellow of two things: He forgot the *Mayor* in front of that *Maude*. And the *Magnus* behind *Millie*.

And what does he know about me being happy?

I lean a little closer to the door to hear the rest.

"The press conference will be held on Wednesday," says Mayor Maude.

My stomach somersaults. If the press conference is happening Wednesday, that only leaves two days to save the playground! I grab my bag of posters and rush to the front door!

"Just the person I was looking for!"

It's Josephine Draper walking toward me. "I've been trying to catch you to tell you something."

"Sorry, I can't talk right now!" I tell her just as the doorbell rings. "Atticus and his big brother are here!"

Something really important is happening, and we have to get to the playground fast!

7

Icky, Sticky Bubble Gums

When we get to the playground, I'm out of breath! But that doesn't stop the words from popping out of my mouth!

"What? A press conference in two days?" repeats Lunchbox. He takes a squishy ball out of his box and hands it to Atticus.

"Yep!" I say, and start pulling the posters out of my bag.

"Poppy Anne, hand me that tape, will

you? Guys, we can't just stand around. I need everyone doing something and FAST!"

I walk over to the pirate ship and hold up the sign. I wait for Poppy Anne to bring me the tape. But she doesn't.

"Slow down, Millie Magnus. Let's think for a minute," she says.

I huff out a breath. "Fine. I'll get it myself." Then I puff, "It's not like I haven't been doing everything all alone, anyway."

"I think Poppy Anne is right," chimes in Lunchbox. "Maybe we're moving *too* fast. I can hardly keep up with what we're really doing."

"Take a deep breath," suggests Atticus. Which I know I should. But I don't.

Poppy Anne makes a stack of the posters before the wind blows them away. "Maybe it's time we just talk to Mayor Maude?"

"Or that Longshmellow guy," Lunchbox adds.

"I knew it." I throw my hands on my hips. "I knew it. Knew it. Knew it!" My voice grows louder and louder.

"Knew what, Millie Magnus?" asks Poppy Anne.

"You guys were *never* serious about saving the playground!" I shout.

I see my friends exchange a look. And it's quiet, like when lightning strikes the air and you're just waiting for the thunder to pound.

"Okay, I've had it," begins Lunchbox. "Millie Magnus, we can't help you save the playground. Maybe we'll try to save it on our own. But we can't work with you anymore."

"Ever since you named yourself mayor, you haven't listened to any of us," adds Poppy Anne.

"Well, that's because you guys haven't listened to *me*." I point both thumbs to my chest. "*I'm* the mayor. And that means *I'm* in charge."

"That's not what being mayor is all about, Millie Magnus," Poppy Anne snaps back. "You're supposed to be leading us, not bossing us around."

Poppy Anne hops on her bike. "Let us know when you're ready to work together, Millie Magnus. Come on, guys, let's go." Lunchbox puts on his helmet and walks over to Poppy Anne and his bike. But Atticus doesn't move.

"Are you staying?" Lunchbox asks him.

Atticus nods. He stands beside me as Lunchbox and Poppy Anne pedal away.

I wait until they're out of sight before a single tear drops from my eye. Then lots of others follow. I sit down on a swing. It's the same one my dad used to push me on. Atticus sits down next to me.

"You remember my dad, don't you, Atticus?"

He smiles. "Like that time he tried to teach you how to skateboard? Remember how you both ended flat on your bottoms?" Atticus and I start laughing until I let out a loud snort. And then we laugh a little more.

"I bet you miss him," says Atticus, looking down at the ground. "I do."

The tears start to wash my face again. "Yeah. I miss him," I say softly. "This playground was our favorite place. That's why I've been going bonkers trying to save it!"

"We like this playground, too, Millie Magnus. It's the bossiness we don't like."

Atticus reaches for my hand. He gives it a squeeze.

"Thanks for being my friend, Atticus."

"Thanks for being my friend, too, Millie Magnus."

Maybe I do need to be better at listening. I need to apologize to everyone. I'm just not sure how. But if I don't, I might lose more than the playground. I could lose my friends, too.

8
The Cheese Stands Alone

When I get home, I go straight to my room and shut the door. Then I take apart the pretend playground made of LEGOs. What's the use? I'll never be able to do this on my own. I'm all out of ideas. And pretty soon, I'll be out of time, too.

I lie on my bed and stare up at the ceiling. That's when a sweet warm smell dances into my nose. I'd recognize freshly baked gingersnaps anywhere.

Josephine Draper walks in with a plate of those yummy things. I try not to act excited. But the truth is, it's just what a lonely mayor needs.

"Cookie?"

My nose answers for me. "Sure."

"Want to talk?" she asks.

"Not really," I say back.

"Okay. I'll take the cookies and go."

"Fine," I say on second thought. "You can stay. I mean . . . it would be nice if you could. I guess I could use someone to talk to."

"Oh no. Something the matter?"

"Turns out I'm terrible at being mayor."

"Is that so?"

My mouth is full of cookies. "Yep."

Josephine Draper sits down next to me. "May I ask what or whom you are mayor of?"

A big gulp of cookies goes down.

I wish Josephine Draper had brought some milk, too. "The playground. Well, saving the playground."

"Hmm. You are the mayor of saving the playground?" she asks.

"It's a big job, I know," I assure her.

"Interesting."

"Wanna know something else that's interesting?" I ask.

"Go right ahead..."

I sigh. "Everyone abandoned me."

But Josephine Draper doesn't believe me. "That doesn't sound like something your friends would do."

I'm just as surprised as she is. "That's what I thought!"

She asks, "Are you sure nothing else happened?"

"Like me being bossy, which didn't happen."

"You certain about that?"

"Okay. Maybe it did," I admit.

"Ah. That will do it." Josephine Draper takes a bite of cookie, too.

"It doesn't matter, anyway. Now my friends don't want to help save the playground anymore." I look away from Josephine Draper.

"In my experience, I've learned there's strength in numbers," Josephine Draper says. "Mayors are not very strong leaders without the help and ideas from their team."

"How do you know so much about being a mayor, seeing as you've never been one?"

Josephine Draper winks. "I spend lots of time listening to a very smart one."

I wink back because that was nice of her to say about Mayor Maude.

"Can I ask you one last question, Millie Magnus?"

"Okay," I say.

"Why do you need to be mayor of saving the playground?"

That's easy for me to answer. "If a

playground is going to be torn down, then it needs to be saved. The mayor is in charge of making sure it gets saved."

"Ah. I see." Josephine Draper stands up. "Well, things are not always what they seem. The only way to find out is to communicate. Perhaps you should talk to Mayor Maude about the playground."

"Tried it. She's too busy tearing it down."

"Perhaps, Millie Magnus, you should try again." She offers me another cookie. "I need to get back to work." Then, as she leaves my room, she says, "Talk to Mayor Maude."

I roll my eyes two times in a circle. What good would talking to Mayor Maude do, anyway?

9
S-O-R-R-Y, I'm Sorry

The next day, while I'm in my room all alone, I decide I need my team back. And the best way to do that is to start apologizing.

I stand in front of my mirror and start practicing my *I'm sorrys*. That's when Poppy Anne, Atticus, and Lunchbox barge into my room.

Lunchbox is out of breath. "Millie . . . Magnus . . ."

Atticus hunches over.

Poppy Anne plops down on the floor.

"Whoopee! I'm so glad you guys are here," I cheer. "I was just about to come find you!"

Lunchbox takes a giant swallow of water and puts the bottle back in his lunch box. "We have some really bad news."

"Oh boy." I sit on my bed and think about crawling back into it and pulling the covers over my head. I don't think I can handle any more bad news.

"We were walking past the playground just now and ... and ..."

"Deep breath," says Atticus.

But Lunchbox can't get the words out.

Poppy Anne jumps in to finish his sentence. "And there was a super-tall guy there holding a clipboard and wearing a hard hat and neon vest."

I stand up and put my hands on hips. "Mr. Longfellow," I say.

Poppy Anne takes a deep breath before she continues. "Worst of all . . ."

I brace myself and plant my feet firmly on the ground.

". . . there's a bulldozer parked next to the slides!"

Lunchbox shouts at the thought of it! "Noooooooo!" So do I! And Atticus, too!

"Millie Magnus, this is our last chance. If we work together, we might be able to save the playground before it's gone. Forever. But we have to act. And fast!"

"I agree!" I tell them. "But first . . ."

I look each one of them right in their eyes.

My friends all look at one another, then at me.

I gulp. Then talk. "I'm really sorry. For all the bossy stuff. And I am really upset with myself about how I treated y'all. I hope you can forgive me. Moody Bubble Gums together again?"

"Moody Bubble Gums together again," they all say.

I put on my blue rain boots with the little chickens on them and head to the door. "I just need a few more minutes. I also need to apologize to the Real Chill Pickles. Starting with Greta Perez."

10
Can't Judge a Book

I'm a little bit scared to apologize to Greta. I've never said *I'm sorry* to a cool big kid before. But I'm excited to see Greta's house.

I bet she has really cool bunk beds with the most fashionable sheets and matching curtains. She probably has a jumbo collection of friendship bracelets from all her millions of friends. Or a secret stash of clothes from Poppy Anne's mom, straight from Paris!

I tell Josephine Draper I'm going next door and walk up Greta's steep driveway. Her mom is tinkering around in their yard.

"Hello, Millie Magnus! It's so good to see you. How are things?"

I want to tell her "bad." But I don't have time to explain why. Plus, now that the Moody Bubble Gums are back together, I feel like we might be able to save the playground!

"Sometimes I'm up, sometimes I'm down, Mrs. Perez. Right now, I'm somewhere in between."

Mrs. Perez grins. "I get it," she says. Then adds, "If you're looking for Greta, she's upstairs in her room. Feel free to go inside."

My stomach does a little flip. I flop my hand on it and remind it why we are here. "You do want to save the playground, don't you?" I whisper to it. "Okay, so relax. We're all right." I keep walking to the front door and slowly open it.

If you didn't know, the funny thing about neighbors is someone can live next door to you, and you can have no idea what the inside of their house looks like until you're walking up the stairs to apologize. I don't know what I expected for a Real Chill Pickle, but so far things look pretty normal. This makes me feel less nervous. But as soon as I make it to Greta's bedroom door, I go back to being not so sure again.

I knock, then wait for a gust of sparkles and amazingness to come flying out of her room when she opens her door.

Instead, it's just Greta with a book in her hand.

"Oh, hi, Millie Magnus. I wasn't, like, expecting to see you here."

That makes two of us not expecting something. I don't say this, of course. I just think it in my head.

I walk into Greta's room, and it's not so sparkly at all. It's actually dark, except for the blue-and-purple glow from her lava lamp.

There's a light blue yoga mat in the middle of the floor.

I take a deep breath. Greta's room smells like my Grandma Sookie's purse. But not in a bad way. *Peppermint*, my nose tells me.

Greta smiles like she knows what I'm doing. "That's the scent from my favorite room spray. It helps me when I need, like, a chill moment."

Greta has books everywhere. Tons

on her bookshelf. Another stack sitting next to her bed. And her desk is covered in them.

"You like to read?" I ask.

"*Love* to read," says Greta. "People think being cool is all about fashion. I like that, too. But I really love a good adventure. When I'm in need of one, I read."

I put this away in my head under "Things to Tell the Moody Bubble Gums Later."

Hanging on Greta's walls are posters in all sorts of bright colors. They say things like:

You shine!

Don't stop until you're proud.

Be kind.

Off in a corner is a reading nook.

"I have one of these! It's in my mom's office! It's my all-time favorite place to curl up with a good book." There is a cage underneath Greta's desk. I inch closer to look inside.

"A guinea pig!" I squeal. It's furry with a big round body and even bigger round eyes. Its ears are teeny-tiny, and its long white whiskers look like they tickle!

"Her name is Pancake." Greta opens the cage and takes the guinea pig out. "Or Tortita. That's 'pancake' in Spanish." She kisses Pancake's nose. "She's bilingual."

I don't ask because I already know that means Pancake speaks English *and* Spanish.

"Having a guinea pig for a pet must be pretty cool," I say.

"Well, just like having a pet chicken." Greta smiles. "But I'm sure you didn't come over to talk pets. Did you, Millie Magnus?" Greta takes a seat on her bed.

"No," I say a little bit quieter than I wanted to. "I came over to say I'm sorry."

I take another big deep breath. "I'm sorry for not listening when you tried to give ideas for the posters. And screaming at you. And, well, being bossy. Like, not in a nice way."

"Wow," says Greta. "That's cool of you to apologize, Millie Magnus."

"I have one more important thing to tell you," I say to Greta.

She nods like she's listening.

It takes a minute before my mouth is ready to start talking.

Finally, I say, "The playground is really important to me. It's where I made lots of special memories with my dad. Now that he's gone, I don't want those memories to go away." I pause, then keep going. "I'm afraid if the playground is destroyed, my memories of him will be destroyed, too." I'm proud of myself for saying that out loud.

Greta motions for me to sit down next to her. And I do.

"Thanks, Millie Magnus. Apologizing is no easy deal. You did great. I feel better, too. And I'm very sorry about your dad."

Greta puts her arms around me for a hug. I put my arms around her, too.

"So what's happening with the playground?" asks Greta. This surprises me. Mostly because I thought the Real Chill Pickles were too old to care about playgrounds.

"It's still going to be destroyed," I say. I really want to beg Greta and the Real Chill Pickles to help us. I want to tell her it's really important we act fast. But the words stay in my mind instead.

"Any extra space on the playground-saving team?"

I light up. Bright! Like Greta's lava lamp.

"For you?"

"And the other Real Chill Pickles," Greta adds.

"Y-E-S, yes!" I holler. "Maybe we could be co-mayors this time," I suggest.

"Or we could just all work together as a team," Greta responds.

"I like the sound of that," I say. "The Moody Bubble Gums and the Real Chill Pickles are back! We're going to make the best team this time around!"

I jump up and do my little happy dance! "Say, Pancake, how do you feel about chickens?"

Greta and I both laugh and laugh until our tonsils hurt.

11

No Rain, No Rainbows

On the day of the press conference, the Moody Bubble Gums and the Real Chill Pickles are outside Extra Spicy's coop working together.

Chance and Izzie have the real good idea of painting giant planks of wood and making them into billboards. Not the real kind. But the kind we can take to the park with us.

Lunchbox and Atticus and his big brother go door-to-door and organize more kids from the neighborhood to help pass out flyers.

Greta writes a really great speech. "Just in case we have the chance to give one," she says.

And Poppy Anne brought *Save the Playground* buttons.

"What a great idea, Poppy Anne. These look amazing!" I say, pinning a bunch to my shirt.

Then I make sure Extra Spicy and Pancake have snacks. And help out where I'm needed.

Plus, someone's gotta keep our plates of freshly baked gingersnaps from ever going empty.

"This sign is ready to go!" I say, wiping the hot-pink paint from my hands onto my shorts and passing the sign over to Izzie.

"I think we're ready to march to the playground," says Greta, admiring my sign.

The sky lets out a loud rumble, and the wind blows a stack of flyers into the air.

Poppy Anne takes a sniff. "Uh-oh! Smells like rain."

Greta looks at me. "Don't worry, Millie Magnus. We won't let anything get in the way of saving our playground."

I smile. Things are better now that we're working together. Much better! Until that Josephine Draper comes outside.

"Millie Magnus, may I ask what's going on here?" Her question tells me she hasn't read any of the signs.

"Simple. We're doing just what you said I should do." I put my hands on my hips. I point my chin up to the gray sky. "We're going to communicate with Mayor Maude at the press conference."

Josephine Draper's eyes get big. "I'm afraid that's not a good idea, Millie Magnus."

"Guys, let's load up the wagons! We're

ready to march!" shouts Poppy Anne from across the backyard.

I pick up a box of buttons. "Sorry, Josephine Draper, but we're going to stop this tearing-down-the-playground business once and for all."

"I think you will not," says Josephine Draper, trying to take the box out of my hands.

RUMBLE! RUMBLE! CRACK! The thunder claps louder than before.

"Millie Magnus, that is not the best time or place to talk to Mayor Maude."

I squint my eyes at Josephine Draper. Lightning strikes from a spot in the sky.

"But this is what you said we should do." I feel my eyes fill up. And then a prickle of water streams down my cheek.

"I'm sorry, Millie Magnus. You simply cannot crash a press conference from the mayor. You will have to speak with her later. Perhaps after the announcement."

"After the announcement?!" I cry. "But it will be too late then!"

"I've said all I have to say. It's time you and your friends bring everything inside before it starts pouring."

But it's too late. Rain comes crashing down on us all. And I don't even have on the right pair of rain boots. I'm wearing my regular black pair. They're so big around the legs that water always comes inside them when it rains.

Within minutes, my toes feel squishy and wet inside my boots. I slosh over to Extra Spicy's coop and grab him and

Pancake. My friends gather posters, signs, flyers, and buttons. We start to bring all our wet stuff inside my house.

Chance's eyes droop as he watches the paint slip off our billboards and into the muddy grass.

"Come on," Greta tries to say to Chance, but the rain is loud now. "They're too big to bring inside!"

"What now?" asks Atticus once we're all standing in my hallway outside Mayor Maude's office. "All our hard work is ruined!"

I look down at the puddle beneath my shoes. "I don't know," I say.

Just then, I hear the front door close and the sound of shoes squeaking. The steps get closer and closer. Then I see Mayor Maude.

"Millie Magnus, Josephine Draper? What's happening here?" Mayor Maude's raincoat is soaking wet. Our march was ruined by the rain. But so was her press conference.

Josephine Draper was right. It's time I talk to Mayor Maude. I try to be brave. Even though my insides don't feel brave at all.

Greta leans closer to me. "You've got this, Millie Magnus. We can do this together."

"Mom, there's something I need to talk to you about," I say. I want to say more, but the words feel stuck in my throat.

But Lunchbox says what I can't. "Mayor Maude, the kids of the neighborhood don't want the playground torn down."

"It's where we go to have a good time," adds Poppy Anne.

"Together," says Atticus.

"And it's really important to all of us." Greta looks at me, then back at Mayor Maude. "Especially Millie Magnus."

I begin to stutter. "It's . . . It's . . ." But I keep trying. "It's where some of my most special times with Dad happened. Like where he taught me how to rock climb. And where we used to swing together."

I pause, then keep going. "It's where we always went when I was having a bad day. I can't imagine bad days without him *and* the playground." My insides must be feeling braver now because I don't even cry when I say this.

Mayor Maude kneels so she's the same height as me and most of my friends. "There seems to be some confusion here," she says to all of us. "We aren't tearing down the playground. That's not the plan at all!" She takes my hands and puts her forehead to mine. "Oh, Millie Magnus. You must have been awfully upset all this time thinking the playground would be gone forever."

"Awfully awful," I say.

"I know how much the playground means to you all," Mayor Maude says to my friends. "Some of *my* most special times have been watching all of you grow into such wonderful kids there. And of course, Millie Magnus, watching you and your dad play together. If I could frame those memories to hang, I would." The way Mayor Maude looks right now, I can't see her tearing the playground down in my wildest nightmares.

Josephine Draper rests her hand on top of Mayor Maude's shoulder. It's like her hand is saying, "Everything is going to be okay, Mayor Maude."

"Thank you, Josephine." Mayor Maude stands up tall again. "You just reminded me. Could you please bring me Mr.

Longfellow's blueprints? I have something I'd like to share with Millie Magnus and her friends."

Josephine Draper leaves and comes back with a huge light blue paper that's rolled up tight.

Mayor Maude unrolls the blueprints. "When I first hear something is going to change, it's a little scary for me, too. But if I think about *why* something is going to change, I often find it's for a very good reason. And sometimes that reason..."

Mayor Maude lays the gigantic drawing on the ground in front of us. "... is to make it BIGGER and BETTER!"

My friends and I all look at one another. Then our eyes light up bright. Our smiles shine like neon lights.

On the drawing are more than shapes and lines.

There's a slide that looks miles high. A brand-new pirate ship in the middle of a splash pad. Sea creatures are swimming with towers of water shooting out of their mouths. There are obstacle courses and things that look like they'll spin round and round. There's a skateboard park and a stage big enough for fashion shows. Concerts even! And a set of swings with seats big enough for big kids or even a dad who likes to swing, too.

"It's perfect," I say so quietly, I'm not sure anyone else hears me.

But Mayor Maude does. She gives me a hug. "Exciting, isn't it?"

I grin. Then nod. It sure is!

12

All Together Now!

The sun is sparkling. The park is filled with people with flashing cameras. Lots of them! Newspeople line up waiting to interview Mayor Maude. The Real Chill Pickles and the Moody Bubble Gums stand behind Mayor Maude, Mr. Longfellow, and me as we hold a giant set of scissors.

"ONE! TWO! THREE!" chants Josephine Draper as we cut the thick red ribbon.

"WHOOPEE!" I shriek as my friends

and I run to explore our new playground. We've waited for what seems like forever for this day to arrive. I grin as wide as my mouth will let me.

"I think that means you like it!" Mayor Maude smiles.

"I don't like it. I LOVE IT!"

"And to think," begins Josephine Draper, "all this time you thought this park was going to disappear! And it just got bigger and better!"

"Well, perhaps," I say in my best Josephine Draper voice, "someone should have told me otherwise." We both laugh! Josephine Draper laughs because she did try to tell me. I laugh because I did a great job sounding just like her!

Mr. Longfellow walks toward Mayor

Maude and me. He's holding a camera. "I'd love to get a picture of the two of you and all your friends. It will be a special photo to remember the grand opening of the new playground."

"I like that idea, Johnny," says Mayor Maude. "Millie Magnus, can you gather all your friends and meet us in front of the playground sign?"

"That's easy. HEY, Y'ALL, PICTURE TIME!" I yell. "LAST ONE THERE'S A BROKEN EGG." I turn to Mr. Longfellow. "That part gets them moving."

"I'll have to remember that." He laughs.

In front of the sign, the Real Chill Pickles lock arms with one another. Then they lock arms with the Moody

Bubble Gums, too. All the kids from the park gather around. Josephine Draper tinkers with the camera on the tripod. Mayor Maude and Mr. Longfellow hold up the blueprint of the playground. Before I join the picture, I look at everyone. The day is almost perfect. But something's missing.

"Millie Magnus, almost ready?" asks Josephine Draper.

"BAWK!" I hurry toward Extra Spicy and pick him up.

"We wouldn't dare take the picture without you, Extra Spicy! Now I am," I shout back to Josephine Draper.

She sets the timer on the camera. "All right, everyone in place!"

I scramble to find a spot to stand. That's when I hear Mr. Longfellow whisper something into Mayor Maude's ear. She laughs with her whole tummy, like he's really funny.

One of my eyebrows goes up. And the other goes down. There's only one person she's supposed to laugh with like that. ME! I decide to stand between my mom and Mr. Longfellow.

"Everyone, cheese on three!" Josephine Draper runs to her spot just before the flash goes off.

"All together now!" she shouts.

"CHHHEEEEEEEEEEEESSSSSE!" we say, making funny faces!

After the picture, I run to look at it on the camera screen. I laugh! My friends and I all look silly. Extra Spicy looks like he's shaking his tail feathers! Josephine Draper just barely made the picture! Then I squint my eyes and use them like they're binoculars.

Everyone, and I mean EVERYONE, is looking at the camera. Except Mayor Maude and Mr. Longfellow.

"Why are they looking at each other?"

I whisper so I'm the only one who can hear what I said. But I decide to keep both eyes on that Longfellow guy for the rest of the day. Maybe longer.

I stop thinking about Mayor Maude and Mr. Longfellow when Josephine Draper walks toward me with Popsicles.

She hands me a purple Popsicle and Mayor Maude an orange one.

"So what happens to Mayor Millie Magnus now?" asks Mayor Maude.

I had almost forgotten about that part of me. "Well, she decided she likes just being a kid on the playground with her friends."

"Trust me, some days I wish I could be a kid on a playground, too!"

"What's stopping you?" I ask.

Mayor Maude thinks about this for a few seconds. "I suppose nothing."

"Wanna swing?" I ask.

Mayor Maude tucks one of my crinkles behind my ear. "I always want to swing with my favorite Millie Magnus."

"Mom," I say. "I'm your only Millie Magnus."

"That's right," she says.

Mayor Maude walks with me to the brand-new swing set. It's nothing like the old swing set. Each swing has two parts—a small swing that's connected to a bigger one—and I know why. I look up at Mayor Maude. "So kids can swing with their dads," I say.

"Or moms," she adds. This makes me happy by a lot, a lot.

"I'm very proud of you, Millie Magnus. And all your friends."

My Popsicle starts to melt faster than I can eat it. I take a big lick of it before I answer. "Proud? But what did we do? We didn't *really* save the playground. Since we had your plans mixed up and all."

"I like the way you put that." She laughs. "Mixed-up plans or not, you all stood up for what you believed in. That takes courage. As for the mixed-up part, that's easy to fix next time with a little communication."

"That's what Josephine Draper said!"

"Smart lady," Mayor Maude says, winking.

"Maybe on some days," I admit.

Mayor Maude takes a big bite of her

Popsicle. "You know what else makes me proud?"

I take a huge chomp of my Popsicle, too. "What?" I squeak just as the coldness goes straight to my brain!

"All the change had you really scared. But it seems you're conquering that fear."

I take a moment to think about it.

Maybe I am. In fact, there are lots of little things that change around me all the time. Like how my hair switches with the weather. Or the stuff Lunchbox puts in his lunch box. Even Extra Spicy looks a little different each day. And then I think maybe I'm not so afraid of change.

Maybe that's because with all the things that are different, there are lots of things that stay the same. Like how I feel about my friends. And how they feel about me. And Josephine Draper. That lady and her fancy strange smells aren't going anywhere.

Here's something else I learned. This whole mayor gig comes and goes. Just look at me. I went from mayor to just being a kid again. But lucky for Mayor Maude, she's got a gig that will never change. No. I'm not talking about her being mayor. I'm talking about her being my mom. That's one thing that's for S-U-R-E, sure!

And I, Millie Magnus, am very glad about that!

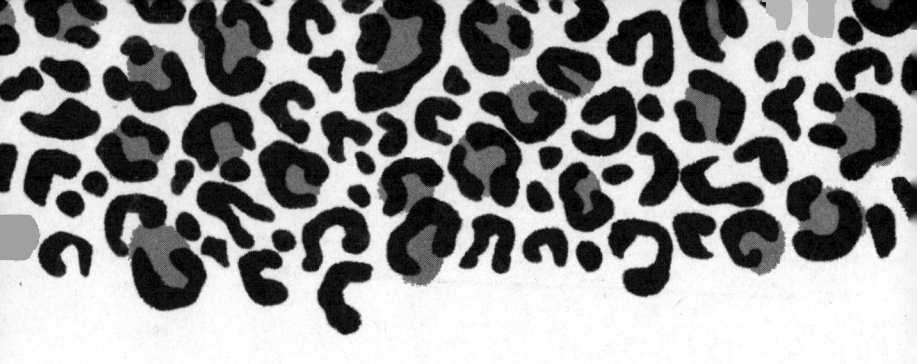

Millie Magnus's Marvelous, Mostly Mismatched Fashion Tips

1. On Socks . . .
They don't have to match! Stripes on one foot, zigzags on the other! Polka dots on the right, pineapples on the left! Perfect.

2. On Accessories . . .
Accessories are tiny cheerleaders. Sunglasses, bracelets, a tiny chicken in your pocket—they're like your outfit saying, "YOU'VE GOT THIS!"

3. On Leopard Print . . .
If you didn't know, leopard is a neutral. That means if you want to wear it with neon,

you can. Camouflage? You can. Doughnuts, hamburgers, or my favorite, lightning bolts? You ABSOLUTELY can. And should.

4. On Rain Boots . . .
They're not just for puddles—they're for POWER. If your boots go squelch-squelch when you walk, then you're unstoppable. Bonus points if they are hot pink and glittery, or covered in lightning bolts. (Mine are both. Obviously.)

5. On Sunglasses . . .
I prefer them over headbands.

MILLIE MAGNUS
★ IS NOT JEALOUS ★

COMING SOON!

★ ABOUT THE AUTHOR ★

BRITTANY MAZIQUE discovered from an early age that most of the characters in her favorite books did not share her skin color. So, she just reimagined them that way instead. She is the author of *The Little Mermaid: Adventures on Land* and *Delphine Denise and the Mardi Gras Prize*. Brittany lives outside of Washington, DC, with her husband, Edward, and her two daughters, Millie and Margaux.

@BRITTANYMAZIQUE

★ ABOUT THE ILLUSTRATOR ★

EBONY GLENN is the illustrator of a number of books for children, including *Speak Up* by Miranda Paul, *Not Quite Snow White* by Ashley Franklin, *Mommy's Khimar* by Jamilah Thompkins-Bigelow, *Twelve Dinging Doorbells* by Tameka Fryer Brown, the Hex Allen series by Jasmine Florentine, and many more. She lives in Georgia with her family.

EBONYGLENN.COM
@ARTSYEBBY

DON'T MISS MORE MILLIE MAGNUS IN

LOOK FOR
MILLIE MAGNUS
★ IS NOT JEALOUS ★

COMING SOON!